THIS BOOK BELONGS TO

Rosie

March 2021   Lockdown.

LADYBIRD BOOKS

UK | USA | Canada | Ireland | Australia
India | New Zealand | South Africa
Ladybird Books is part of the Penguin Random House group of companies
whose addresses can be found at global.penguinrandomhouse.com.

www.penguin.co.uk   www.puffin.co.uk   www.ladybird.co.uk

Penguin
Random House
UK

This book was first published in the USA as *PAW Patrol: Count on the Easter Pups!* by Random House Children's Books, 2018
This UK edition published by Ladybird Books, 2020
001

Printed in the UK
A CIP catalogue record for this book is available from the British Library

ISBN: 978–0–241–45538–8

All correspondence to:
Ladybird Books
Penguin Random House Children's
80 Strand, London WC2R 0RL

SPRINGTIME ADVENTURES

It's almost time for the Adventure Bay Easter Egg Hunt. "You can count on the PAW Patrol and our friends to get things ready," says Ryder.

**Rocky finds ONE big basket.
"Don't lose it – reuse it!" he says.**

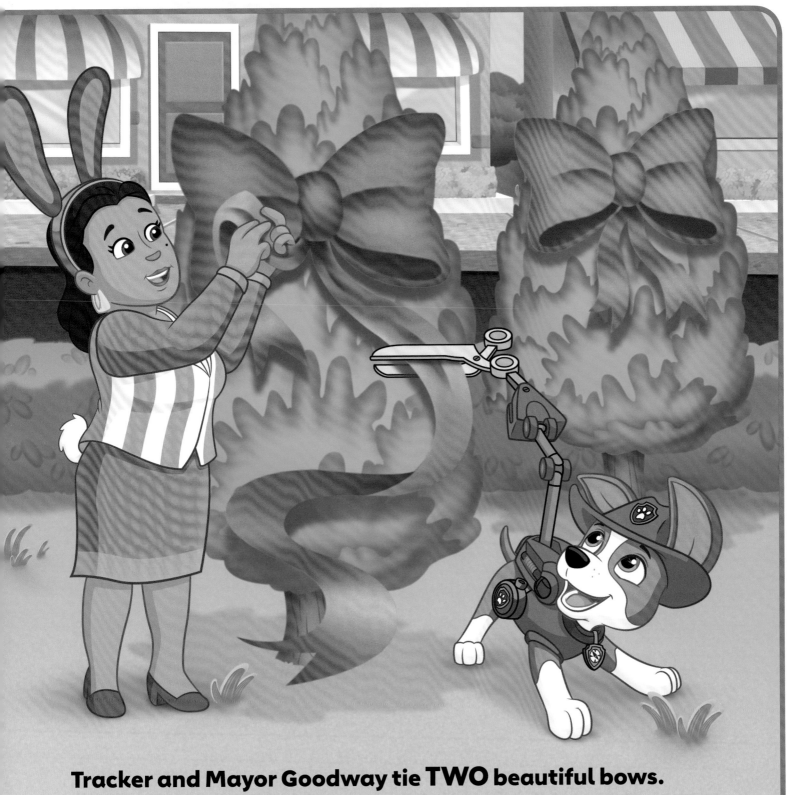

Tracker and Mayor Goodway tie TWO beautiful bows.
"This will be the best egg hunt ever," says the mayor.

Marshall and Everest water **THREE** big, colourful flowers.
"We're ruff-ruff ready for the egg hunt!" says Marshall.

Rubble plays with **FOUR** hopping friends. "You can't have an Easter party without adorable bunnies," he says, with a giggle.

Mr Porter shares **FIVE** bags of yummy jelly beans.

Chase sniffs SIX sweet treats.

Rocky has **SEVEN** bowls of bright dye.
"I'm egg-cited to start decorating!" he says.

EIGHT pups do the perfect Easter dance – the bunny hop!

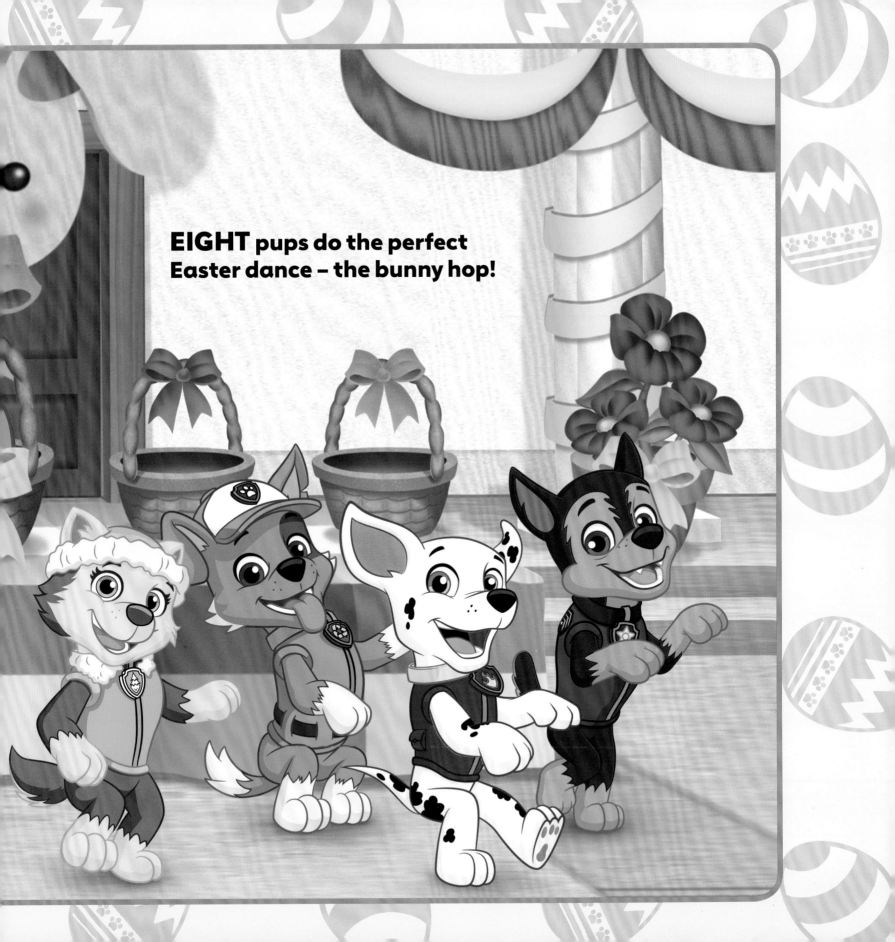

Skye hangs **NINE** fluttering flags.
"This party is about to take off!" she says.

"There are **TEN** eggs hidden here," says Ryder.
"Let's find them all!"

"HAPPY EASTER FROM THE PAW PATROL!"

ADVENTURE BAY SPRINGTIME QUIZ!

How well were you following the pups' adventures? Can you answer these PAWsome questions?

1. Who found the big basket?

A. Skye

B. Ryder

C. Rocky

2. What did Tracker and Mayor Goodway make?

A. A big mess
B. A lot of noise
C. TWO beautiful bows

3. What dance did all the pups do?

A. The bunny hop!
B. The fan-dog-go
C. Ballet

4. Who had a lovely time playing with bunny rabbits?

A. Mayor Goodway

B. Rubble

C. Nobody

5. What did Mr Porter share with everybody?

A. Jelly beans

B. Carrots

C. Easter eggs

6. How many cupcakes did Chase find?

A. None

B. Six

C. A million!

7. What were Marshall and Everest watering?

A. Flowers

C. Ice creams

B. Bunnies

8. What did all the pups find in the end?

A. Carrots
B. Shoes
C. Easter eggs